POLAR PERIL

SHOO RAYNER

ORCHARD BO

D0266819

CHAPTER ONE

"This has to be the coolest place on Earth!" Axel Storm said excitedly.

He was looking round the amazing entrance of the Ice Hotel, where his family were staying. The hotel was just like its name suggested – it was made entirely out of ice!

"Actually, it's much cooler outside," said Axel's dad, tapping the thermometer on the wall. "It's only minus five degrees in here. Out there it's minus twenty-two!"

"Apparently the hotel melts in summer and they have to rebuild it every winter," said Mum, as she hung her clothes up in the heated wardrobe. "It's like sculpting a new piece of art each year."

Their room was beautiful. Even
the beds were made of ice, but because
they were covered in deep layers of
reindeer fur, they were actually very
warm and cosy. The icy walls and
ceilings twinkled and glowed with
thousands of tiny light bulbs.

Axel's mum and dad were rock stars. Their band, Stormy Skies, had recorded twenty-two platinum-selling hits in eighty-three different countries around the world. They spent most of their lives travelling, performing concerts and meeting their millions of fans.

They had come to the Arctic to make a music video for their new song, *Northern Lights*. They wanted to film the video beneath the real Northern Lights – the spectacular natural light show caused by night-time solar activity in the far, frozen north.

"Now Axel, we'll have to start filming as soon as we see the Northern Lights," Dad explained. "We've arranged for you to go to Celebrity Kids' Club while we're working."

"What!" Axel wailed. "You know I hate Celebrity Kids' Club. Santa's grandson was there last time I went. He's not nice like his grandad. He kept putting snowballs down the back of my neck!"

The Storms were very rich and famous. But even though they were richer and more famous than you can imagine, they still tried to live normal lives.

"We want to protect you from all the newspaper and magazine reporters," Mum said calmly. "They're so desperate to get a story about the band, they've even followed us this far north. You can't grow up normally if your picture is in the papers all the time."

Just then, Axel heard a strange noise.
"That sounds like something scratching
at the ice window," said Axel, going
to investigate. He was right! Outside
there was a large dog, scratching at the
window.

Axel watched in amazement. With
claws, teeth and a hot, pink tongue,
the dog scratched and bit and licked
a hole in the ice. When the hole was
big enough, it popped its head right
through.

"He's got something round his neck," said Axel. "And my name's written on it!" Axel removed the tube that was attached to the dog's collar and opened it.

"There's a message inside," he said. "It's from Uncle Stanley!"

Glacier Research Centre, Arctic Circle

Hi Axel,

I heard you were in the area.
I could really do with your help at
the research centre. I'm here all on
my own. It would be nice to have
some company.

Write your reply on this letter and
Jasper will bring it back to me. If you
say yes I'll come over to pick you
up tomorrow.

Lots of love,
Uncle Stanley

"I didn't know Stanley was up here,"
Dad said, sounding surprised. "The
last I heard he was doing research on
penguin poo in Antarctica."

"So, can I go?" Axel asked in his
sweetest voice.

"Hmmm… It might be a bit
dangerous," said Dad.

"It's *scientific research*," said Axel.
"That's much better than Celebrity Kids'
Club – it will be really *educational*."
Axel knew the word *educational* always
impressed his parents!

"But what about the photographers?"
said Mum. "Archie Flash from *Celebrity
Gossip Magazine* will do anything to get
a story about you."

"I don't think even *he* would travel
to a lonely glacier to get pictures of me,"
Axel pointed out.

"Oh, all right," said Mum. "After all, Uncle Stanley *is* the most sensible of all your uncles. I suppose he'll be able to keep you safe and sound."

"Woo-hoo!" Axel cheered. He wrote *yes* on the letter and put it back in the tube. Jasper panted expectantly as Axel snapped the tube onto his collar.

"Off you go, boy," Axel whispered, stroking the dog's thick, deep fur. "See you again tomorrow."

He couldn't wait!

Then Dad picked up the phone and called the hotel reception desk. "Hello. Could you send someone to fix a hole in the window? It's freezing in here!"

CHAPTER TWO

The next day, Uncle Stanley arrived on a sledge in a flurry of snow. Jasper led his pack of yelping huskies. He wagged his tail and barked loudly when he saw Axel again.

"Hello, Jasper!" said Axel, patting the dog.

Uncle Stanley ruffled Axel's furry hood. "My goodness!" he exclaimed. "Haven't you grown?"

Axel sighed. Why did grown-ups always say that?

Mum and Dad hugged Uncle Stanley and told him he'd better look after Axel properly. They didn't want him having one of his wild adventures and ending up in the newspapers again.

"The research centre is really remote," Uncle Stanley explained. "No one ever goes there. Certainly not news reporters."

Uncle Stanley bundled Axel onto his sledge. "Do you know how to get the sledge going, Axel?" he asked.

"I think you say something like, *Mush!*" said Axel.

As soon as the huskies heard the word they leapt to their feet, barking and yelping. Before long they were on their way, speeding across the frozen wastes of the north.

From far behind him Axel's parents'
voices hung in the air.

"We love you, Axel. Be good! See
you soon!"

Axel leant back in the sledge as the
huskies pulled them through the endless
white wilderness. Without an engine,
using only dog power, he felt as though
they were leaving the twenty-first
century behind. They were so far from
any kind of civilisation that they might
just as well have been on the Moon.

Uncle Stanley pointed over Axel's shoulder. "There's the glacier, and that's the research centre over there. It's not much, but it's home."

The glacier was an enormous river of ice that slowly flowed down from the mountains into the sea. In the distance, Axel saw brilliant blue water dotted with icebergs.

The research centre looked like a tin shed that had been dropped from the sky into the middle of nowhere. It had to be one of the loneliest places on Earth.

"Come on, I'll show you the glacier," Uncle Stanley said, when they'd unloaded everything and untied the dogs from the sledge.

Inside the the building, Uncle Stanley opened a door and flicked some lights on. A long, gently sloping tunnel lay before them.

The tunnel opened into a cave. The roof glowed with a strange, greenish-blue light. Axel couldn't work out where they were. The sound of rushing water filled the space around them.

"We're right under the glacier!"
Uncle Stanley explained. "There's a
million tons of ice above us. If we stood
still for long enough, we'd be crushed
into strawberry jam!"

"Woah!" Axel had a moment of panic. "Are we safe?" he asked.

"Oh, sure," Uncle Stanley said. "The glacier moves very slowly, maybe thirty or forty centimetres a day. That's one of the things I measure here." He showed Axel some of the electronic equipment that was hung around the cave.

"The ice moves slowly down to the sea where it breaks up and makes icebergs. Global warming is making the glacier shrink. Soon there won't be any icebergs in the sea at all."

"What are those gurgling noises?"
Axel asked.

Uncle Stanley sighed. "That's the
sound of melting. Each year, the ice
melts more quickly. The glacier is
riddled with tunnels of fast-flowing
meltwater, a bit like those water flumes
you get at swimming pools."

"That sounds like fun!" Axel smiled.

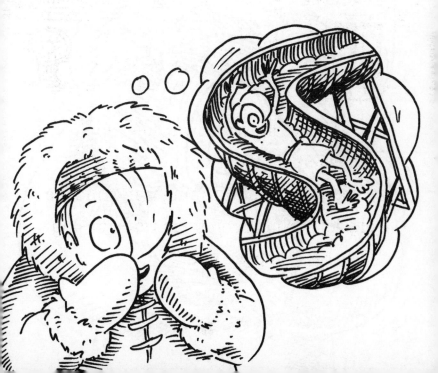

"You don't want to fall down one of those tunnels," Uncle Stanley warned. "Who knows where you'd come out? You'd probably freeze to death or drown along the way. So watch where you tread!"

Axel shivered at the thought.

CHAPTER THREE

Outside in the freezing cold, Axel had the strangest feeling that they weren't alone.

"There are polar bears round here," Uncle Stanley explained. "Part of my job is to save the environment for the bears. If they have cubs to protect, they might attack you, so always be on your guard."

Axel felt a little scared. "W-what if they come towards you?"

Uncle Stanley hung a survival pack on Axel's belt and showed him the contents.

"This is a Bear Scarer! If you feel threatened, pull the string and throw it. After three seconds it makes a very loud bang, so cover your ears! Most of the time the bears run away."

"And if they don't, I run away instead, right?" Axel laughed.

"This is serious." Uncle Stanley frowned. "If a polar bear sees you running, he'll think you're his lunch. You have a far better chance of surviving if you stand absolutely still. And don't let it off for fun," he added. "It's so loud, it could set off an avalanche. You'd be crushed in the ice or buried in snow."

Axel gulped. "This is a dangerous place!"

Uncle Stanley showed Axel a bigger tube. "If the banger doesn't work, this makes a massive red smoke screen. You can also use it to attract attention if you get lost."

Uncle Stanley pointed at the survival pack again. "You've also got two days of rations and a sheath knife. There's a saw on the back of the blade so you can cut blocks of ice to make an igloo," he added.

Uncle Stanley showed Axel how to stack blocks of ice on top of each other, in an inward curving spiral. In no time at all they had built a perfect igloo.

Inside the igloo, protected from the
the biting cold wind, it was quite cosy –
like a mini Ice Hotel! Uncle Stanley and
Axel sat down to get their breath back.

"Coo-ee!" A voice outside startled
them both.

"What the…" Uncle Stanley made
for the doorway, but Axel beat him to it.

Whump! Outside, a brilliant flash of light almost blinded him.

"Archie Flash! What are you doing here?" wailed Axel.

Archie Flash, the photographer for *Celebrity Gossip Magazine*, had followed Axel and his uncle all the way from the Ice Hotel.

"I've got some great pictures of you with my new digital camera," he said. "Our readers will love them. They're such great fans of yours, Axel. They want to know about everything that you do."

"But…" Axel was lost for words. "But…how did you get here?"

"They taught me arctic camouflage and survival skills when I was in the army. You were very easy to follow." Archie held up his camera. "My new camera takes video, too. Our readers will love to see you on our Celebrity Gossip Video website."

"But you can't just come and photograph Axel like that," Uncle Stanley complained. "It's not right!"

Archie Flash looked confused. He held up his hands and looked around him with a quizzical expression. "I'm just taking pictures of the snow," he smiled. "I can't help it if Axel gets in the way!"

All his life, Axel had been followed by photographers. If Axel sneezed, they wanted a picture of him for their magazines.

Maybe one day I'll get a bit of peace and quiet on my own, Axel thought.

But this was not that day. Axel stared in horror as a huge, white creature appeared over the ridge, behind Archie.

"Don't look now!" Axel hissed. "But there's a polar bear right behind you!" He felt a primitive fear clutch at his throat, and his heart began pounding.

"I'm not falling for that old trick!"
Archie laughed.

"Walk over to us, slowly and
carefully," Uncle Stanley ordered.

The huskies saw the bear and
began howling.

The expression on Archie's face changed. Slowly, he turned round. The bear stood on top of the ridge. It licked its lips and stared at Archie.

Whump! Fear made Archie click his camera. The flash exploded in the bear's eyes. It stood up on its back legs and roared with rage.

"*Rooaaar!*"

"Arrgh!" Archie yelled, and ran towards Axel.

The bear lumbered straight at them, its vicious teeth bared and its massive claws pounding the ice.

Axel forgot all of Uncle Stanley's advice. He turned and ran with Archie towards the glacier.

Axel never heard Uncle Stanley shouting for him to stand still.

As they ran, Axel grabbed the Bear
Scarer from his survival pack. He pulled
the string and threw the banger over his
shoulder.

The bear's pounding paws thudded
ever closer. Three...two...one...
B-O-O-O-O-M!

CHAPTER FOUR

The ground gave way beneath Axel's feet, as if he were dropping in a high-speed elevator.

It was a while before Axel understood what had happened. The exploding banger had left a loud, ringing sound in his ears. Slowly he became aware of the rushing noise around him and realised the terrible situation he was in.

The banger had fractured the ice beneath him. He'd fallen into an icy meltwater tunnel. Axel was zooming down a perfect tube of ice, at what seemed like a thousand miles an hour, with no idea where he would end up.

From the yelling and the roaring behind him, Axel guessed that Archie Flash and the polar bear were close behind him.

The tube twisted, turned and spiralled down the length of the glacier. It went on for ever, getting steeper and faster all the time. The strange, eerie blue-green glow of the ice whizzed past him all around.

Ahead, he saw the tube split in two. Thinking he was going to crash into the middle, Axel shut his eyes tight.

"Arrrghh!" he screamed, as the ice funnelled him down the left-hand tube.

Soon, Axel could only hear himself yelling. He realised Archie and the polar bear must have gone down the right-hand tube.

The glow grew brighter as he raced through the frozen labyrinth. Was that a light at the end of the tunnel? Was he going to survive after all?

The cold hit Axel in the face as he shot out of the tube and flew through the air.

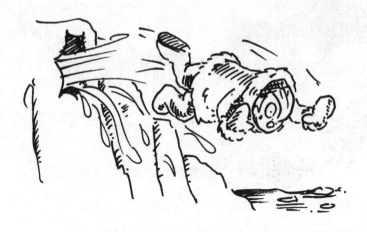

Below, the azure blue sea rushed towards him. He knew he'd die in minutes if he fell into the freezing water.

"*Oof!*" Axel landed on soft snow, but it still hurt. He groaned, picked himself up and took in his surroundings.

The end of the glacier was a huge wall of ice rising up from the sea. He'd been thrown out of the tube like a ski-jumper, and had landed on the snowy surface of an iceberg that had just split away from the glacier.

With a terrible, wailing scream,
Archie came flying out of another tube.
He curved gracefully through the air
and landed – *thump!* – on another
iceberg close by.

Seconds later, the polar bear appeared close behind. It scratched and scrambled at the side of Archie's iceberg, but it couldn't get a grip on the slippery surface. The enormous beast tumbled and turned and fell into the water with an enormous splash.

Archie and Axel held their breath. Moments later, the bear broke the surface. It shook its head and, looking very disgruntled, swam slowly back to the shore.

CHAPTER FIVE

Axel's iceberg slowly drifted in the current. Archie's iceberg followed just behind.

Even now, Archie was taking pictures of Axel.

"They'll discover that stupid camera one day," Axel muttered to himself. "And they'll be able to see how I perished out here on my own – all lovingly filmed in high definition by Archie Flash!"

Axel knew he had to pull himself together. He made a survival plan.

He cut blocks of snow and built himself an igloo for shelter. He had two days' emergency rations – enough to keep him going until someone came looking for him. Archie would have to look after himself.

The night came quickly. Axel looked out at the star-studded sky. He'd never seen stars look so bright. Each one shone like a brilliant diamond.

Then the weirdest, most wonderful
thing he had ever seen happened.

Giant sheets of shimmering light, like
glowing, velvet curtains, danced across
the night sky. The sea reflected the
greens and pinks and purples.

"The Northern Lights!" Axel
whispered in awe.

Across the water, Archie cheered
and whooped on his iceberg as nature
put on her most spectacular light show.
Archie and Axel were like two specially
invited guests.

When the lights died down, Axel
climbed into his igloo, closed his eyes
and waited to discover what his fate
would be.

CHAPTER FIVE

"I don't believe it!" Dad wailed. "Axel has done it again! Two million people have watched his video online in the last twenty-four hours. Only three people have viewed our new music video."

"It's amazing!" Axel said, watching the footage for the hundredth time. "Archie filmed everything!"

The video showed the polar bear attack, the great slide down the ice tunnels and, best of all, there was film of Axel standing awestruck under the Northern Lights. Mum and Dad's song, *Northern Lights*, had been added as a soundtrack, making the song their latest platinum-selling hit.

Axel's Polar Peril

CELEBRITY GOSSIP MAGAZINE WEBSITE

"We never got to see the Northern Lights!" Mum complained. "We had to play in front of a green screen and they put the Northern Lights effect on afterwards."

As Mum watched the part where Axel was rescued by a helicopter, she gave Axel a hug. "You could have died out there! I don't know how you get yourself into these adventures. I wish you could just be an ordinary boy."

"I *am* ordinary," Axel insisted. "I just have a very *extraordinary* uncle!"

CELEBRITY GOSSIP MAGAZINE

AXEL STORM IN ARCTIC RESCUE

Axel Storm was safe and sound today after surviving a night of peril on an Arctic iceberg. Our reporter filmed the brave young lad as he set off a bright-red smoke flare which was spotted by an eagle-eyed rescue helicopter.

The President of the Arctic Nations has asked Axel to become an ambassador to the youth of the world, to draw attention to global warming in the Arctic.

"AXEL IS A FINE EXAMPLE TO ALL YOUNG PEOPLE," he said.

Axel was unavailable for comment.

His uncle said, "That boy sure knows how to survive!"

By ace reporter, Archie Flash

SHOO RAYNER

COLA POWER	978 1 40830 264 4
STORM RIDER	978 1 40830 265 1
JUNGLE FORTRESS	978 1 40830 266 8
DIAMOND MOON	978 1 40830 267 5
DEATH VALLEY	978 1 40830 268 2
SEA WOLF	978 1 40830 269 9
POLAR PERIL	978 1 40830 270 5
PIRATE CURSE	978 1 40830 271 2

ALL PRICED AT £3.99

Orchard Books are available from all good bookshops,
or can be ordered from our website: www.orchardbooks.co.uk,
or telephone 01235 827702, or fax 01235 827703.